The Friendship Fairies Go to School

The Friendship Fairies Go to School

LUCY KENNEDY

ILLUSTRATED BY
PHILLIP CULLEN

Gill Books

Gill Books
Hume Avenue
Park West
Dublin 12
www.gillbooks.ie

Gill Books is an imprint of M.H. Gill and Co.

Text © Lucy Kennedy 2020
Illustrations © Phillip Cullen 2020

978 07171 89670

Edited by Sheila Armstrong
Printed by BZ Graf, Poland
This book is typeset in 14 on 28pt, Baskerville.

The paper used in this book comes from the wood pulp
of managed forests. For every tree felled, at least one
tree is planted, thereby renewing natural resources.

A CIP catalogue record for this book is available from
the British Library.

5 4 3 2

CONTENTS

To my sisters Anna and Gemma.
I love you both.

CHAPTER ONE

'Dive bomb!' shouted Holly Dixon, racing off the diving board and jumping into the swimming pool.

SPLASH!

Water spilled over the edges of the pool, drenching her two sisters, who had been enjoying the last of the summer sun.

Her whole family was used to getting splashed at this stage. Some of their neighbours

even kept an umbrella with them at all times, just in case Holly was using the pool that day! Last week, she had bounced so high off the diving board that she had fallen out of the treehouse and landed on Mr and Mr Snail's roof below. They were quite old and had got a terrible fright!

Holly was wearing her red and black scuba-diving outfit, which was confusing for the local ladybirds, as they often mistook her for their cousin. Her dark-brown hair had grown long over the summer, and she now liked to wear it half up with a colourful scrunchie that matched her outfit.

'Holly,' moaned Emme, who was sitting beside the pool. Luckily, the book she was reading was waterproof.

Emme had grown a bit taller over the summer and she felt very grown up. This year, she would be starting with a brand-new class at the senior school. Emme was very organised – she had bought herself a noticeboard to make a homework schedule and had even tried to plan her packed lunches for the full year ahead! As excited as she was, she was also nervous about going to a new school on her own, as her two sisters would be staying behind in The Magic Manor.

Little Jess wiped the water from her eyes and stuck her tongue out at Holly. Her hair had become even fairer from being in the sun all summer, and she had a few new freckles on her nose. Jess was coming out of her shell as a person but, being the youngest of the three girls, she still got away with mischief. Her family often found things she had 'borrowed' hidden under her pillow. It could be a new bobbin, a doll or some sweets. Holly called Jess 'Sticky Fingers', which made Jess very cross!

Mr Dixon had spent the early part of the summer renovating the treehouse roof, and he had cleverly installed the swimming pool for the family. It was about the size of an adult human's little finger!

It had taken him a week to carve it out of a big conker shell, and then they had to wait for the rainwater to fill it. The sun heated the pool naturally and made it feel like a warm, cosy bath.

Jess sometimes added bright blue bubble bath that she bought with her pocket money. When Emme was on her own in the pool, she played loud music. She loved Elf Rock, which was quite noisy and involved a lot of head-shaking. It was quite a sight to see, especially when she had her headphones on!

As Holly splashed in the pool, a Butterfly Taxi pulled up outside the Barns treehouse. Ollie, Hugo and Harry Barns had gone to Germany in early June to stay with their German cousins. They had been helping their uncle, who was a vet and owned a clinic for injured insects. Now it looked like the Barns Boys were back in town.

Holly was secretly pleased, because she liked one of the triplets, Harry. He had a kind smile and a good sense of humour … but she could never tell her sisters because they were supposed to be enemies.

'*Guten Tag!*' shouted Harry across the fence.

'More like jet lag,' yawned Ollie, and Hugo sniggered. They carried their suitcases inside, tripping one another up as they went.

Mrs Dixon came out to the pool just as the sun was beginning to go down. Over the summer she had taken some well-earned time off from her work in the spy unit. She had been investigating farmers who were not recycling properly. She used fairy-future dust on them, which gave humans nightmares about what the environment would look like if they didn't look after it. The farmers had soon changed their ways!

'Right, girls,' Mrs Dixon said. 'One final swim and then in you come to wash and have dinner. It's the first day back to school tomorrow, so we all need an early night.'

'Yes, Mummy,' said Emme and Jess at the exact same time, waving at her.

'Coming, *Gemma*,' said Holly, trying to be funny by using her mum's first name. She got into trouble every single time she did it, but she quite simply could not resist!

'Holly!' said Mrs Dixon. 'I mean it, now. We've talked about this before – no more cheek or you can all come in straight away.' And with that, she turned on her heel and went back into their treehouse.

The sisters looked at each other and quietly got into the pool for a final swim. 'Why does

Holly always try to ruin everything for us all?'
thought Emme. Jess made sure to splash her
cheeky sister extra hard.

After a few minutes, they got out and
headed inside. Holly wrapped her towel around
her head like a turban, as she was convinced
that it helped her hair to dry straight. Then
they got into their fairy-jamas and ate dinner
together.

For dinner, their mummy had made scrummy-wummy pie, which was purple pastry full of magic vegetables, chicken and gravy. Mr Dixon had made some iced buns the night before, so they enjoyed those for dessert.

And then it was time for bed. They were so tired from swimming all day long that Jess almost fell asleep while brushing her teeth.

Before she got into her bunk bed, Emme polished her golden medal from The Magic Manor. Last year, at her graduation ceremony, her teacher, Ms Ava, had been talking to a very handsome man who had mysteriously disappeared. Emme had meant to figure out who he was, but she had been having such a good time all summer that she had forgotten! 'Maybe somebody at my new school will know who he is,' she thought as she fell asleep.

Emme woke up later in the night with a pain in her tummy. She felt nervous about starting a new school, so she went into her parents' room.

Her parents were talking about work and getting ready for the morning, but when they saw Emme's worried face they let her sit down on their sleigh-bed.

'It's very normal to be nervous, love,' said Mr

Dixon. 'You don't know what you don't know. But

when you know, you'll know. You know?'

Emme looked confused but nodded politely.

She knew that her dad was trying to help her,

but he sometimes got his words jumbled up!

Mrs Dixon laughed and joined in. 'What Daddy is saying is that it is okay to feel nervous about a new situation. But you'll get to know your new school soon, and then you'll feel right at home.'

The three of them chatted for a while and together they decided that while not knowing can be a little bit scary it can also be exciting – like having an amazing new dream waiting for you after a long day.

'But no matter what,' Mrs Dixon finished, 'you can always talk to us about what you are feeling. Always share what you are feeling with someone you trust, because it helps,' she said.

Emme went back to bed and fell asleep immediately and began to dream a lovely dream about unicorns. Outside the window, Alex the

Owl was twit-twooing on the windowsill. No
one knew how, but when the Dixon girls were
unhappy, Alex just knew, and he would appear at
the windowsill to lull them to sleep.

CHAPTER TWO

The following morning, the alarm went off early.

The alarm, of course, being Richie the Rooster, who was two hundred and seventy-two. He had lived on the tree branch all his life with his wife, Harriet. They had been married for one hundred years, and he still bought her flowers.

Every morning, Richie would take a drop of watery fairy-honey, clear his throat, stick his tummy out, close his big brown eyes and open his beak. The sound of his alarm was a mixture between a tractor starting its engine and a very loud, shouty sneeze!

A-ROCK-A-ROON-GUH-CHOO!

Inside the treehouse, Emme was so excited that she bounced out of bed, dying to try on her new uniform and sparkly black shoes. Now that she was starting at the senior school, she had to wear a white shirt and navy dress. The red jumper was optional for when it got cold. She hummed away to herself happily as she got dressed. Suddenly, a flying purple pillow whacked her right in her face!

'Holly!' she said, annoyed.

Her sister was not a morning person at all and made sure that everyone knew it! As Holly hid grumpily under her blanket, sighing loudly, Jess slid off her bed and landed right on her feet. She then got dressed and sneakily put one of Holly's pink hairclips into her pocket.

The girls arrived downstairs and could hear the creamy porridge bubbling away on the stove. Mrs Dixon had the honey and warm milk ready to pour on top. It was very important to eat brekkie as it really did set you up for the day.

'Remember now, girls, a butterfly can't fly without nectar, can it?' Mr Dixon reminded them most mornings.

'Dad!' Jess would say, 'We are little fairies, *not* butterflies!'

After their tummies were nice and full, and Jess's morning burps were fully out, they brushed their teeth, used the bathroom, collected their backpacks and flew out the front door. Literally!

It was a nice bright Monday morning with a light breeze, which always made flying a bit more fun because it added some wind beneath their wings. But on really windy days, some of the younger fairies and elves had to put tiny little pebbles in their school bags so that they wouldn't drift off like balloons! The older children always minded the little ones, though. That was the most important part of the **fairy-safe code** – kindness always comes first.

At the entrance of The Magic Manor, Emme hugged her two little sisters tightly and waited outside until she saw them fly into their classroom. Her new school was down the road and she suddenly felt very alone.

She took a deep breath, trying to focus on what her parents had said. 'I can do this,' she decided, and started flying away. She didn't see them, but Holly and Jess were watching her from the classroom window until she flew out of sight. They were a tight little threesome at times – when it mattered.

Emme headed off down the road and on the left she saw a big building – it was five times the size of The Magic Manor! Before she could think any more negative thoughts, she quickly flew up to the big brown door. A sign on the door read: **Belle-Spell Castle.**

Emme gulped. She could feel the butterflies in her tummy again. Taking a deep breath in, she raised her hand and slowly pushed the heavy door open ....

When she stepped inside, she could hear the hustle and bustle of students walking, flying, trotting, buzzing, crawling and leaping up and down the long corridor.

'Oh dear,' she thought. 'How will I ever get used to this?' Everyone seemed so busy and unfamiliar, and she didn't recognise anyone from her neighbourhood. She felt quite stressed until she saw a red door marked **OFFICE**.

When she put up her hand to knock, the door opened by itself. A lovely older lady with big brown eyes, rosy cheeks and pink hair tied up loosely with a piece of celery was sitting at a very messy desk. Emme read her name tag, which said Mrs Boon.

'Hello, Emme,' she said, 'I've been expecting you. Come on in.'

Emme was quite taken aback by this. 'Um, excuse me, but how do you know my name?' she asked politely.

'Well,' Mrs Boon replied, 'I know all the students' names. It's my job to know. You're here because you are special. In this school, everyone is especially unique and uniquely special.'

This gave Emme a warm feeling in her heart. This lady seemed so calm and kind that she was immediately put at ease. She breathed out in relief – probably much louder than she had realised.

Mrs Boon smiled. 'Don't be nervous, Emme,' she said. 'It's okay to feel a bit jittery on your first day, but it's how you manage those jitters that's important. Starting at big school can be a bit scary, of course, but you will settle in very quickly here.'

Emme nodded, hoping that Mrs Boon was

right! Perhaps everything really would start to seem more familiar.

'Now, take this note down to classroom seven. That's where Sir Prize will be. He's your teacher, Emme. You're very lucky,' she whispered, blushing. 'He's the most magical person I know. He lives in a house surrounded by unicorns! Oh, you'll learn so much from him. Good luck, love, and remember – my door is always open if you are worried or just fancy a chat.' As she left, Emme heard her add quietly, '… or if you have any **cake**.'

Emme flew back down the corridor. She
finally found classroom seven and flew inside.

She looked around quickly at the faces in front of her. There were all sorts of creatures in her new class – fairies, elves, animals, and even a werewolf with braces on her teeth.

Everyone looked very cool and calm and she began to get the jitters again. 'I'll stay near the window,' she thought. It seemed cosy over there and she could try to catch a glimpse of her sisters.

She plonked herself down beside an elf. She had long, black hair and a sulky face. She was leaning on her elbow and looked tired already.

'Hello,' said Emme and introduced herself.

'**Whatever**,' said the elf, and she turned to another girl on the other side of the table and started talking to her.

'Okay …' thought Emme, a bit shocked by the girl's rudeness. She started to get that weird feeling in her tummy again, but then she was distracted by the other students running to their seats.

A few moments later, the classroom door swung open and nothing could've surprised Emme more (other than Holly coming in disguised as a male teacher).

It was the mystery man from her graduation! He had a pierced ear and a ponytail and was as handsome as she had remembered. He was wearing a black suit with a waistcoat and hat which looked more suited to a royal wedding than teaching a class of students!

He also had a lead with him, which he unwrapped from around his hand and left on the desk. Emme was wondering if he had a pet of some sort and then remembered that Mrs Boon had mentioned unicorns – how cool! She had only ever seen one from a distance as they were extremely shy creatures.

'I'm Sir Prize,' he said formally and bowed to the group. 'You are all very welcome to my class. I hope that we can enjoy the year together and learn lots.'

He sat down at his desk and smiled. 'Now

then, who wants to learn some real magic?'

CHAPTER THREE

Meanwhile, in The Magic Manor, Ms Ava had arrived into the big, noisy classroom. 'Well, hello, everyone,' she said with a warm, friendly smile. 'Welcome to a brand-new year! I hope that you're all as excited to work together and learn new skills as I am.'

The class nodded at each other. 'Okay, let's settle down now and get organised. Let's split into two groups – the younger students on the left, and the older students on the right.'

Holly looked over at Jess, who was singing 'Baby Troll' quite loudly and doing all the moves. 'Jess!' Holly whispered, trying to catch her eye, but Jess was in her own little world.

'**JESS!**' she said loudly, and only then did Jess stop mid-song with her hands on her hips. 'Listen to Ms Ava!'

'Oh,' said Jess, and casually followed the others across the classroom. Holly watched her walk away, concerned that her little sister was going to get in trouble soon. The two sisters wouldn't be in the same group this year, so Jess would have to step up to the plate and learn some manners!

Ms Ava settled the younger ones at the craft table. They were going to design rainbows using listen-markers, which would follow your instructions when you asked them to draw something for you.

Miss Jess was already pushing through the group with a narky face, trying to get her favourite colour marker. Holly decided that instead of interfering, she could sort it out for herself. Jess was used to people always doing things for her. She would have to grow up and start listening!

'Righto,' said Ms Ava, kneeling on the ground in front of the older students and encouraging them to do the same. She had to politely ignore the chairs and desks skidding loudly across the room when the new student, a French elephant, tried to kneel down. It was pretty loud!

'So, everyone, we are going to step things up a bit for you this year. How are we all feeling?' she looked around at the class. 'Excited and ready?'

There was total silence, except for one quick sneeze from the Swedish llama, who didn't seem to notice and just kept staring ahead through the glasses on her nose.

Holly pretended that there was dirt on her purple high-tops and started to examine them closely with her leg in the air. After a few seconds, she realised that Ms Ava and the class were all staring at her. She lowered her leg slowly and blushed. How very embarrassing!

'Holly? You usually have a lot to say, about … pretty much everything,' Ms Ava said with a glint in her eye.

'Um, yes, I do,' fumbled Holly. 'I feel, um, amazing and ready for the challenge?' She tried to look serious.

'Good answer,' said Ms Ava as Holly breathed a sigh of relief. She had promised her parents that she wouldn't cause any trouble or get up to any mischief on day one.

'This year is all about knowing the difference. Your first assignment is **black lies** and **white lies**. There is a *big* difference, you see. A black lie is when you are not telling the truth to help yourself. But a white lie is when you bend the truth slightly to help another person. Do you all understand?'

'Got it,' said Holly confidently. 'I'm on the case and have just the thing for it.' She stood up and started unpacking her things.

'What exactly are you doing, Holly?' asked Ms Ava. 'I haven't finished.'

'Oh, sorry. I'm off to find some liars and trap them with **THIS**.' To the class's surprise, Holly produced a red fishing net and some jellies.

'That is *not* the way to do this, Holly,' said Ms Ava, indicating that Holly should sit down. 'I mean, by talking and listening to people, you will learn the difference between the two forms of lying.'

She was greeted with blank, slightly confused faces.

'Let's talk about this,' continued Ms Ava. 'Imagine that it is your birthday and your friend has given you a present of a new orange jumper. But you don't like the colour orange. What do you say?'

Holly stood up again to deliver her answer loudly to the group. 'I say to my friend: look, this jumper is manky. Take it away and bring me something nice.'

'No. No, Holly,' said Ms Ava, calmly. 'That is not nice, and they are mean words. Mercy, do you have any idea?'

The French elephant thought for a moment.

'I would say … zank you for zee present, I like it?'

'Exactly,' said Ms Ava.

'But she's lying!' said Holly, furious. Her face always went red when she was annoyed or embarrassed.

'No Holly, she is not lying. She is saving her friend's feelings and not hurting them. Now, I would like you to write down some more examples of white lies. Mercy, you can work with Holly on this.'

'*Mais oui*,' said the elephant.

While they worked away, Ms Ava walked over to the younger group. 'Let's all form a circle,' she said in a kind voice. She noticed that Jess was not listening and instead was talking to herself. 'Jess, can you join the group, please?' she asked.

Jess turned around and realised that the whole class was in a circle and she was not in it. She ran over and joined the group, looking embarrassed.

'We need to learn about **listening ears**,'
Ms Ava continued. 'Listening ears are when we
open our ears and hear what someone is saying to
us,' she said, looking directly at Jess. 'Remember
that our ears want to listen. They like to do their
job properly – so help them! Okay, class?'

'Yes, Ms Ava,' they all replied at the same time.

'Now, I want you to spend all this week
working extra hard on your listening ears.'

After lunch and some reading time, a chime rang to end the class. The two sisters packed up their bags and left together to collect Emme after her first day.

As they approached Belle-Spell Castle, Holly spotted Harry Barns leaving the building. She smiled and flew towards him, but as she got closer she could tell that he was sad.

'Hi, Holly,' he said when he looked up.

'Hi, Harry! Welcome home! Did you like it? Do you speak German now? How were the insects?' Holly blurted out. She had waited all summer to ask these questions!

'Well,' said Harry, taking a step back, 'yes, I did like it, and no, I don't speak German, and I loved the insects …'

Holly opened her mouth again, but Jess put her hand on her arm. She could tell from all her listening practice that Harry still had something to say.

'But,' Harry went on, 'you would be so sad if you saw how some people treat their pets. Some poor insects aren't being given enough food or are being left alone in the cold. I don't understand how people can be so mean. I don't think I want to be a vet anymore.'

Holly could not believe that anyone in the whole world could be unkind to helpless insects. 'Harry, you will be a great vet.'

Harry looked up and smiled sadly. 'Thanks,' he said, before flying away to join his brothers.

A few minutes later, Emme came outside and saw her little sisters. Her whole face lit up when she saw them.

'Well, tell us everything!' said Holly.

'It was alright,' said Emme, trying to sound cheerful as she tucked her new magic wand into her bag before the others saw it. She knew that if they spotted it they would want to try it out.

Emme was feeling a bit blue, but she didn't want her sisters to know this. The new schoolwork she had to do was difficult, and she hadn't had much luck making friends. But she had a plan that involved her new wand …

CHAPTER FOUR

The following morning, the Dixon family woke up very early, before Richie the Rooster had even left his nest, because there was chaos on the roof of their treehouse!

'What is going on up there?' said Mr Dixon, walking out of his bedroom. He was still half asleep as he scratched his head and tummy at the same time.

'I don't know, Daddy,' said Jess, taking his hand and Holly's too. They all went into the

kitchen, where the window was wide open. All
they could see was a cloud of purple smoke.

Holly looked up. 'Hello up there?' she said
bravely.

'Oh, um … hi, Hols, and good morning,
family,' said Emme's voice, sounding out of breath.

'Emme, what *are* you doing?' shouted Mrs
Dixon as she came out of the bedroom. 'I'm

coming up there,' she said, tucking in her pyjamas and flying out the window.

'Oh, Emme!' she exclaimed when she saw what had happened.

'I know,' answered a beautiful white horse, wearing shorts and a T-shirt. It sounded just like Emme! 'I was trying out my new wand, and I've turned myself into a horse by mistake.'

'Not to worry,' said Mrs Dixon, trying her best not to laugh. 'I know this spell, so I can reverse it.' She picked up the wand, closed her eyes, murmured something and – **poof!** – Emme was back.

'Thank you!' said Emme, relieved and a bit embarrassed.

'This wand is a big responsibility, Emme,' said her mum. 'You are not meant to practise any magic outside school. I thought you had to leave the wand in a special safe at night?'

'I know,' said Emme. 'I just wanted to show the other girls that I can do magic. To make them like me.'

'Emme, I understand that it can be very difficult to make friends, but you have to give it time. I know you are a good person, and other people will soon see how great you are too.'

Emme hung her head sadly.

'Now, down you go and get ready for school. I'm going to trust that you understand what I've said about your wand.'

Emme nodded.

'Good girl,' she said, kissing her sensitive little daughter.

'What were you doing?!' asked Holly and Jess at the same time as Emme flew back in the kitchen window.

'She was just horsing about,' said her mum, laughing.

Emme laughed and blushed a little. It was actually quite funny, she thought – just a bit embarrassing!

The girls got dressed, had brekkie and headed to school. Holly and Jess waved goodbye to Emme and flew to The Magic Manor.

That afternoon, it was time for Holly to test out her new understanding of black lies and white lies. She and Holly flew to the meeting spot they had agreed on with Mercy the Elephant. She had a backpack on – and some shades, Jess noticed. Holly's influence must be rubbing off on her.

'Let's go,' said Holly loudly.

'*On y va*,' said Mercy with gusto.

'I love strawberries,' Jess shouted, right into their faces. There was silence. She had just felt the need to be involved!

They headed off together to **Wise and Wiser**, which was a home especially for human old people. Holly reckoned that at least one of them would be a liar!

They snuck in, as sneakily as a small French elephant and two fairies could, and headed for the nearest radiator. They were good spots for fairies, because they could hide behind them and not be seen. The fairy-safe code says that fairies have to stay hidden from humans – unless they are helping a child with a problem, of course.

Sure enough, the room was jam-packed with old folk. They were all talking at the same time, with their eyes closed. 'Bizarre,' thought Mercy.

They were right beside the table where the humans were eating their lunch. They waited and waited, and then Holly heard someone walking over. She was wearing a cook's hat and carrying a ladle.

'How are you getting on with your lunch, Kate? Are you enjoying the egg that I made you?'

'Oh, it's lovely,' said the woman called Kate, looking a bit uncomfortable. 'Thank you so much.'

'Great,' said the cook, moving on to the next group. Holly watched intently, nudging Mercy to make her concentrate. She saw Kate turn to the tiny little lady sitting beside her.

'The egg is actually yucky,' she whispered. 'It's hard and cold, but I didn't want to hurt the cook's feelings. But it's just a **white lie** really, isn't it, Barbara?'

Barbara put her false teeth back into her mouth and agreed with her. 'Yeshhh, Kate,' she said, spitting little blobs of rashers and sausages into Kate's hair. 'No harm done wisshhh a white lie.'

Kate looked up suddenly. 'Barbara, did something just land in my hair?' she asked, feeling her head.

'No, nothing,' said Barbara, avoiding Kate's eyes and staring at her lap.

Holly nodded. 'Aha! Got it,' she thought to herself. 'Kate told a white lie to save the cook's feelings, and Barbara told Kate a black lie by not telling her the truth about spitting in her hair. I can tell the difference now.'

Behind Holly, Jess was staring across the room and listening carefully to a chat between a child and her granddad. The kind old man was telling the little girl that he wasn't feeling well and that was why he lived in this old folks' home. The little girl looked very sad. She wanted her granddad to come to her house and play with her toys, but he couldn't.

Jess felt sorry for her. There were far too many adults in the room for her to help the little girl – even though most of them had their eyes closed, they might still spot her.

Then the little girl began to cry, and Jess decided to take a risk. She flew down to the little girl's ear when her granddad's back was turned and whispered, 'You'll be okay.'

Then she took out a handful of **hug-dust** that she had 'borrowed' from her mum's bag that morning. She sprinkled some of the bright blue powder on the old man's hair.

The little child turned and looked Jess right in the face. She broke into a smile as her granddad turned around and wrapped her in a big hug.

Jess winked at her and flew back to Holly, who was breathing heavily, in shock.

'Jess!' she hissed at her sister. 'You are *not* allowed to break the fairy-safe code, you know that!'

'I know,' said Jess, 'but I had to make sure that little girl knew that someone was listening to her.'

Holly was taken aback. 'Okay, well, I am annoyed … but also proud, because you used your listening ears. I will not tell on you – *this* time!' Holly took a deep breath and exhaled dramatically. 'We're out of here, peeps,' she said to Mercy and Jess. 'That was too close! Much too close. Let's go!'

And with that, they climbed out from behind the radiator and scurried out of an open door. It was only when they were flying back home that Holly noticed Jess chewing a piece of human breakfast cereal.

'Whaaat?' said Jess, shrugging. 'When a fairy's gotta eat, a fairy's gotta eat!'

Holly frowned at her but then laughed to herself.

Later that evening, Holly wrote up her assignment on black lies and white lies and left it at the front door for collection.

While they were having dinner, they heard a big **thud** from outside the treehouse. It sounded like someone or something had flown straight into the tree. 'It's just Peter collecting the homework,' said Mrs Dixon, shaking her head as she scooped up her pasta. 'That pigeon really should start wearing glasses.'

CHAPTER FIVE

The next day, Emme woke up feeling tired. She had not slept well again. She was enjoying her new lessons, and she really liked her teacher, Sir Prize, but the lack of friends was getting her down. Mrs Boon had come by the classroom the day before, but she had left before Emme could talk to her, because somebody was having chocolate birthday cake in the staffroom. Mrs Boon took cake very seriously.

She packed up her bag with a heavy heart and put a smile on her face so that her parents would not worry. She knew that they just wanted her to be happy.

'Come on then, you two,' she called to her younger sisters, who were fighting over a carton of fairberry juice. They both wasted so much time arguing over silly stuff!

'FINE!' said Holly when her mum told her to let Jess have it. Jess had a smug look on her little face as they flew off to together.

When they got to The Magic Manor, the front door was closed and there was a big notice on it.

Poor Ms Ava had been scuba diving with a shoal of clownfish, and she had swum straight into a rock and banged her head! She was fine, but Dr Bear-Butt said to take the day off to rest. She'd be back next week.

Holly was delighted. She truly believed that she worked too hard and needed a day off!

'Now what will we do for the day?' said Jess.

Holly had noticed that Emme had seemed a bit down that morning. 'I have an idea, Jess. I think our big sister might need us,' she said, putting her arm in the air like a superhero.

Jess sighed and followed Holly as she flew off. She knew better than to argue when her sister was in this mood. She also decided not to draw attention to Holly's knickers, which were on the outside of her leggings — and inside out.

They headed for Belle-Spell Castle and made it to the front lawn in time for the first break. Jess could hear the bell ringing and soon the students poured out of the door to have a snack and get some air. After a few minutes they saw Emme on her own with an apple in her hand. She looked sad, Holly thought.

'Let's just watch,' she said. Jess nodded and they found a flowerpot and hid behind some dog daisies.

Holly could see Harry Barns across the lawn. He was playing floating football with the other students. She hoped he wouldn't give up on his dream of being a vet. He was a good guy, Holly had decided, but it was a shame about his brothers, Ollie and Hugo. They were shouting and being very rough. It even looked like they were stamping on the flowerbed!

Emme sat down close to the flowerpot, so her sisters had a great view of her. They watched as a group of students came out to the garden and Emme stood up immediately, eager to see them. She flew straight over to a black-haired elf who was in the centre of the crowd.

'Hi there,' she said, hopefully.

The black-haired elf just looked Emme up and down.

'Um, would you like to play chasing?' Emme tried once more.

'Yes, but not with you,' said the black-haired elf with a mean look on her face. 'I don't like you.'

Holly was very tempted to jump out and shout at the girl, but she knew that she had to let Emme do this on her own. 'Breathe, Holly,' she said to herself. Jess, who was practising her listening, just stared at the mean girl.

'Well, that's very strange,' said Emme confidently. 'How can you not like someone you don't even know?'

The girl looked confused.

'Why don't you give me a chance?'

Emme turned to speak to the rest of the girls. 'I have plenty of friends outside school, but I thought because we are starting a new term, we could all play together too.'

'Okay,' said a pretty fairy in a quiet voice. 'My name is Hazel.' The werewolf with braces on her teeth introduced herself as Cleo, and the three began to chat.

The elf with the black hair looked a bit left out, but then Emme smiled at her. She smiled back, and her face changed when she smiled. She didn't look sulky at all.

'You know, you're right, Emme,' she said. 'I'm Annie, and I'm sorry for being rude. I'm just, well, worrying about a few things at the moment and I was taking it out on you. You seem like a nice person.'

'**She is!**' shouted Holly very loudly from the flowerpot. Then she remembered that they were supposed to be hiding, so she ducked.

The girls all looked around, confused. Where had that come from? After a minute, Emme shrugged. She tagged Annie, saying 'You're it!' and they all ran off, laughing.

'Holly! said Jess. 'You're a naughty girl. You could have got us caught!'

'Oops!' said Holly, laughing. 'Come on, Emme's fine now. Let's go and get some puffy buns!' The sisters flew off together.

When nobody was looking, Emme turned around and blew a kiss to the sky. She could recognise her sister's voice a mile away. 'Good ol' Hols,' she thought. She was the most annoying person that Emme knew, but by far the kindest.

Over dinner that evening, Mr and Mrs Dixon saw a huge difference in their eldest daughter. She was messing and laughing with her sisters again. Mrs Dixon asked the girls how their day had been.

'Really good, actually,' said Emme, smiling happily, 'I've made some new friends. They're nice. Also, as well as turning myself into a horse' – Emme laughed at her own joke – 'I can now help clouds if they are running low on water by saying a magic spell.'

Handy to know, thought Holly, if the Barns Boys were annoying her.

'And,' Emme continued, 'I can make my hair curly or straight whenever I like.' She grinned at her family.

'Not fair!' shouted Holly and crossed her arms. She really wanted straight hair, even though she had beautiful curls.

'Fantastic news, love,' said Mrs Dixon, feeling relieved. Her daughter was back to her usual happy, positive self. 'And Holly?' she asked.

'Great, thanks, Gemma,' said Holly, eating away. Now that Emme was feeling better, she was more concerned with hatching a new plan – Harry Barns had looked like he needed cheering up.

'Holly!' said her mum. 'This is your final warning. I'm Mummy to you. No more cheek!'

After dinner, they had warm rain-showers and got into bed.

Jess sang them to sleep. Tonight's song was 'Be kind, be magical', which she sang loudly with all the hand actions, including blowing kisses to her sisters, until they told her to be quiet.

CHAPTER SIX

It was the end of the first week back at school. There was a real sense of achievement and relief in the air. The weekend was here and everyone, big or small, loved the weekend!

Emme's class were having a party to celebrate at Sir Prize's castle. His actual castle! The class could not believe it when he had suggested it, and now they were ridiculously excited to see inside it.

At playtime they had heard some crazy stories from the older students, who had gone the year before. They heard that not only did he have real unicorns but also a secret treasure room, guarded by a dragon! That gave Emme the heebie-jeebies because she was a bit scared of dragons.

For the party, she had decided to wear her new Elf Rock T-shirt, with jeans and a pink hoodie. Her hair was tied up in a high ponytail with a long purple ribbon. She looked and felt great, because she was happy.

Holly had sat on her bunk bed last night, helping her decide on her outfit. She had also pressed Emme for details about the party, making sure that Emme didn't leave out any piece of info. Emme was so excited that she didn't realise that Holly was plotting something.

Holly had heard all about Sir Prize's pet unicorns, and she thought that this was just the thing to cheer Harry Barns up. If he saw these beautiful creatures, he was sure to decide that he wanted to become a vet after all.

Now, her plan involved herself and Harry Barns getting to the party too! She had sent a midge note to Harry last night, telling him the plan. Midges worked for free (well, free-ish – you had to give them some food) and they would pass notes between the treehouses after six o'clock every evening.

Emme had arranged to meet her new friends Annie, Hazel and Cleo outside the school, where a special bus was picking them up and driving them to Sir Prize's home. Mrs Dixon flew down with Emme just to make sure that she was safe getting on the bus. Then she was off to do some shopping with Jess.

As soon as Emme and her new friends saw each other, they squealed with excitement.

'I almost couldn't sleep!' said Emme to Hazel. 'I still can't believe that we are actually going to a real castle!'

'I know! Me neither,' said Hazel, with shining eyes. She had brought along her pet lizard for the trip, and he looked just as excited.

They chatted as the other students were getting on the bus. It always took a bit of time as they had to lower the bus ramp for anyone who was on all fours, like the donkey and the ants. But nobody minded, as they knew it was important for everyone to be included.

The bus was being driven by a kind lady called Jane. She was well known in the community for her cool glasses with flashing lights.

Just as the bus was about to leave, a strange-looking old couple got on. The grey-haired lady had an odd walk – and was definitely wearing sparkly runners under her dress.

'Just getting a lift to the shops!' said the old man in a creaky voice.

'*Shhh*, Harry,' Holly whispered to the old man as she limped her way to the back of the bus.

The bus drove through a green, leafy forest and up a steep hill. It was a drizzly day, and Emme could see that the plants were enjoying the rain.

When the bus finally turned into a long, dark driveway, all the students went quiet and looked out of the window in awe. There were poles on either side of the driveway and as the bus approached, they lit up and fireworks popped out of them and into the sky!

When they got closer to the castle, they could see that the whole building was lit up in bluc to look like a massive waterfall. **'Wooow!'** said the entire bus at the same time. Even the old couple had stopped whispering to each other and were staring out of the window in surprise.

The bus stopped and Jane led the students up to the huge steps in front of the castle. Once they were all standing on the first step, it started moving! The steps rolled over each other and carried the students up to the massive green front door.

And then it opened.

Standing there was an interesting-looking character called a mookie. A mookie was a mixture of a mouse and a cookie. Its face was round like a cookie with mousey features.

'Come in,' the mookie squeaked. 'Let me take your names and mark them off my list.'

'Oh dear,' thought Holly, thinking quickly. 'I never thought that there would be a list!' She nudged Harry, who was whistling to himself. He was not taking this seriously!

'Och hello, son,' said Holly in her best Scottish accent when they got to the top of the queue. 'We're … um … unicorn nutritionists. We've come to feed the poor aul' unicorn some new healthy treats.'

Harry couldn't look at her in case he laughed. Her accent was terrible! But the mookie didn't look surprised at all.

'Oh good, we've been waiting for you. They're exercising in the rainbow pool at the moment,' he squeaked. 'Go on in.'

'Oh, that's great, thank you, laddy,' said Holly, shocked that this had worked. And with that, the mookie was gone, leaving the strange-looking old couple in the hall.

'Right,' said Holly to Harry. 'The rainbow pool it is …'

In the meantime, the other students were
heading into the main hallway. When they got
inside, the lights went off and music came on.

A single light shone up at the ceiling. Sir Prize was slowly coming down from the ceiling, sitting on a green dragon with pink eyes. Emme couldn't believe it. This wasn't a scary dragon – this dragon looked kind, with big glasses and a wide smile.

'Welcome, class,' said Sir Prize, 'and thank you all for coming to my home.' The dragon glided over to land on the floor and lowered her head so he could gently slide off.

'Let's have a **party**,' he said, and all the

lights came on.

No one could believe their eyes. The entire room had changed. In the middle was a long table covered with delicious food. There were mookies walking around, setting the table, pouring drinks and doing funny poses.

All the students ran over to the table and enjoyed the feast together with Sir Prize, who sat at the top of the table, chatting to Jane.

After they had all eaten and had full tummies, Sir Prize clapped his hands, and the table, the mess, the chairs, everything, disappeared. Gone completely!

'We'll have cake later,' he said, 'but for now, let me show you all around.' They formed a kind of messy line. Everyone wanted to be at the front, but they had to give in to the English hippo, who was very big, bossy and stubborn. She wouldn't move from her spot.

Emme stayed beside her friends as they walked through corridors and looked inside different rooms, each one more interesting than the one before. There was a sewing room, an underwater room, a painting room, a sticker room, a jungle room – a room for everything! In some rooms, the mookies were working away or relaxing by open fires, waving whenever they saw someone.

Soon the students passed a big silver door that had thirty locks on it and a camera that followed the students' every move. 'There's some serious security here,' thought Emme.

'In there,' Sir Prize announced, 'is my very private secret room. I cannot tell you what is inside, because it is top secret.'

'Is it the treasure room?' Annie whispered to Emme.

'No, it's not,' answered Sir Prize quickly, causing Annie to blush. Blimey! He had amazing hearing.

'That's in **HERE**!' he said as he opened the next door. The class gasped. Inside, there was a massive pile of treasure right in the middle of the floor. There were gold and silver coins, big wads of notes and lots of glistening jewels in every colour. The class was mesmerised.

Emme noticed that the green dragon was sitting quietly beside the treasure, doing her nails.

'Thank you, Drailia,' Sir Prize said to the dragon. 'You might check on next door,' he said, winking.

Emme's ears pricked up immediately. 'Ooh, I have to find out what is behind that door,' she said to herself, but the class was already moving on down the corridor.

'And *finally*, you can all meet my favourite animals,' Sir Prize was approaching the last door in the corridor, which was sparkly pink.

'No one, and I mean no one, is allowed in here – unless a mookie approves them.'

As he turned the handle, the class held their
breath. They had all heard about the beautiful
unicorns and they couldn't wait to see them!

The door opened slowly, and the first thing
the class saw was the old couple chatting away
as they dried the unicorns beside a rainbow pool.
The couple did not even notice Sir Prize, Jane,
and the whole class walking into the room.

'So, you see,' said the old lady, 'yes, there are mean people in the world. They may not know how to treat their creatures properly, but maybe no one showed them how. They need someone like you to teach them the right way.'

The old man was just nodding and patting the unicorn with a blue towel. The unicorn looked very happy. The class watched in awe.

Sir Prize cleared his throat loudly. 'Excuse me?' he said.

The old lady got a big fright and jumped up from her stool, her shawl falling to the ground. It was a little girl! A fairy!

'**HOLLY?**' Emme shouted, shocked to see her sister.

'You know her?' asked Sir Prize in a cold voice.

'Yes,' said Emme, aware that all eyes were on her. She could feel her cheeks getting hot. 'She's my younger sister.'

'Right, then,' continued Sir Prize. 'Why are you here in my castle? With my precious unicorns?'

'Okay, so the thing is–' began Holly.

'It was for me,' said the old man, standing up to reveal that he was actually a young fairy under the fake white beard. 'My name is Harry, Harry Barns. I'm Holly's neighbour and she wanted to remind me why I wanted to be a vet. So we snuck in to see your unicorns. We've been looking after them, though, and they are all very healthy,' Harry finished confidently.

Sir Prize still looked annoyed, and he turned to Holly. 'But how did you get in?'

'I'm sorry, I lied to the mookie,' added Holly, hanging her head. 'I just wanted to help my friend.'

'Well,' said Sir Prize, 'I suppose it was a **white** lie. And, Harry, my unicorns do seem to like you. No harm done, so I'll let you off this *one* time.'

Harry let out a huge sigh of relief.

'Thank you!' said Holly, avoiding the cross

look on her older sister's face.

'**But,**' said Sir Prize, opening a cupboard and taking out two shovels, 'having pets means cleaning up after them.' He led Holly and Harry out into the yard, where there was a big pile of purple unicorn poop. 'The mookies could do with a day off. You two can clean up all this!'

Holly and Harry looked at each other and groaned loudly. They picked up the shovels and got to work.

Meanwhile, Emme and her class spent some time petting the unicorns and then headed back to the hall.

As they stood at the bottom of the stairs, a mookie brought in a massive wibbly-wonky cake. It was filled with fresh strawberries, jam and cream, and it towered over the students.

A door opened and a mookie led Holly and Harry into the room. Their clothes were all rumpled and they didn't smell very nice. Even the English hippo turned up her nose at them.

'Holly!' said Emme, finding her sister. 'Wait till I get you home ...'

'It's okay,' said Sir Prize. 'They've learned their lesson – I hope!'

Holly and Harry nodded so fast their heads nearly fell off!

Everyone began to tuck into big slices of the wibbly-wonky cake. Then, all of a sudden, the doorbell rang, and a mookie went to answer it. Sir Prize looked confused. 'I'm not expecting any *more* unplanned visitors,' he said.

The mookie came back into the room with Mrs Boon.

'I was just in the area,' said the school secretary, 'and I thought that I could smell something …' She was eyeing up the wibbly-wonky cake and licking her lips.

'Of course,' said Sir Prize, laughing. He wasn't surprised. Mrs Boon really did love cake!

After all the excitement, Jane the driver got everyone on the bus and brought them back down the hill, through the forest, and back to Belle-Spell Castle. Parents, grandparents and minders were waiting to bring them home.

'Good day?' asked Mr Dixon, as they flew home to see Mrs Dixon and Jess.

Holly began to tell her dad all about the unicorns, but Emme was distracted.

She couldn't stop thinking about that secret
room in the castle with all the locks … but that
would have to be a mystery for another day!